ROAR!

For Jack, Anna and Natalie
MM

For Tom and Charlie Mumford
and for Siwan
AA

ORCHARD BOOKS
First published in Great Britain in 2006 by The Watts Publishing Group
This edition first published in 2017

3 5 7 9 10 8 6 4 2

A CIP catalogue record for this book is available from the British Library.

ISBN 978 1 40835 554 1

Printed and bound in China

Orchard Books
An imprint of
Hachette Children's Group
Part of The Watts Publishing Group Limited
Carmelite House
50 Victoria Embankment
London EC4Y 0DZ

An Hachette UK Company
www.hachette.co.uk
www.hachettechildrens.co.uk

Margar t Mayo & Al x Ayliffe

ROAR!

Bold **lions** love roar, roar, **roaring**,
While cubs play – racing, chasing,
Scrambling over lionesses and – oops! – tumbling.
So **roar**, bold lions, **roar!**

Wrinkly **elephants** love **mud-wallowing**,
Squishy-squashy! Squishy-squashy! Squelching,
Trunks sucking and – shwoo-**oosh!** – water squirting.
So **wallow**, wrinkly elephants, **wallow!**

Stripy **zebras** love **fast galloping,**

Dumm-dd-dum! Hooves drumming,

Manes rippling, tails flying.

So **gallop**, stripy zebras, **gallop!**

Fierce **tigers** love prowl, prowl, **prowling,**

Through the jungle slowly s l i n k i n g,

Softly creeping, no . . . grr. . . growling.

So **prowl**, fierce tigers, **prowl!**

Tall **giraffes** love stretch, stretch, stretching,

Long necks going up . . . up . . . reaching,

Black tongues flicking, lips leaf picking.
So stretch, tall giraffes, stretch!

Cheeky **monkeys** love swing, swing, swinging,
Hanging, dangling, tightly clinging,

Treetop scampering, calling and screaming.
So **swing**, cheeky monkeys, **swing!**

Plump **hippos** love swim, swim, swimming,
Floating, underwater strolling,
And opening their giant mouths ...waaaahh
...till all their teeth are showing.
So swim, plump hippos, swim!

Spotty **leopards** love climb, climb, **climbing,**
Up tree trunks zipping, sharp claws gripping,
Among the green leaves, crouching, hiding.
So **climb**, spotty leopards, **climb!**

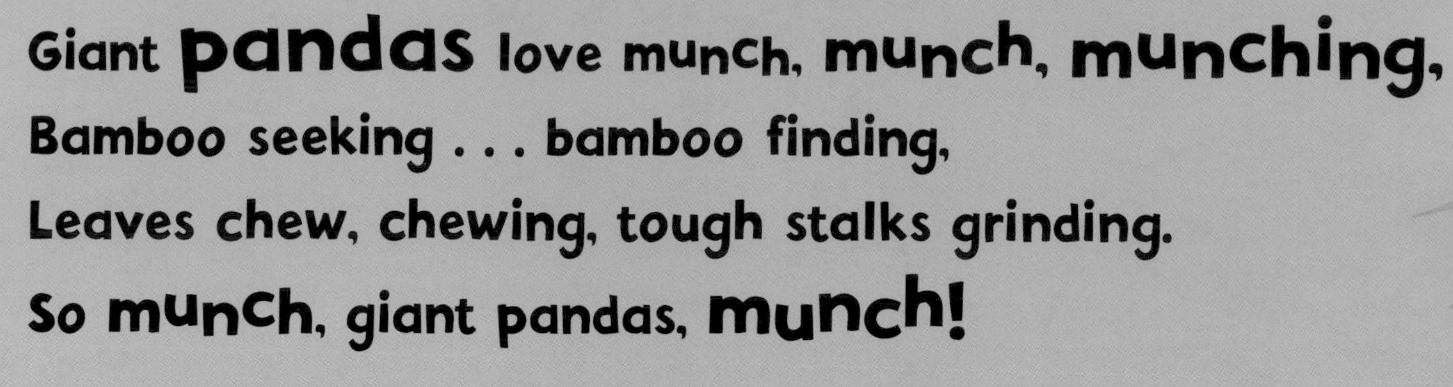

Giant **pandas** love munch, **munch**, **munching**,
Bamboo seeking . . . bamboo finding,
Leaves chew, chewing, tough stalks grinding.
So **munch**, giant pandas, **munch!**

Bouncy **kangaroos** love jump, jump, jumping,
Hopping, bounding and . . . bumpety-bumping!
Little joey in the pouch, eyes peeping.
So **jump**, bouncy kangaroos, **jump!**

Grizzly **bears** love **fish, fish, fishing,**

In fast rivers *splishing, splashing,*

Paws catching, jaws quickly snatching.
So **fish**, grizzly bears, **fish**!

At night some animals love peaceful sleeping,
In a tree, on the ground or jungle floor.
But some are out prowling, hunting and eating,
While . . . wide-awake lions still love to **ROAR!**